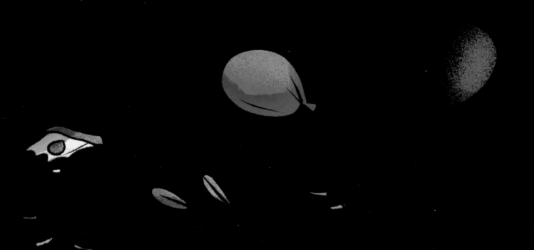

DREAM BIGGER! IMAGINE MORE!

THE IMAGINATION AGENCY

It's Bedtime, but who wants to go to sleep, when your best friend spends the night? Let the partying begin!!!

"Hey, A.J.! It's bedtime!"

Ahh, finally some sleep.

It always starts with a cool breeze.
Which is usually the result
of a dragon's sneeze.

Then there's the flamingos' thundering roar, Which you cannot ignore,

Everyone knows that unicorns party the best.

But the zombies are always fabulously dressed.

If this party gets any crazier,

Okay, I totally have this party under control.

Dinosaurs, turn up
that rock and roll!

Bears, go get the trolls.
Gooberwackies, take your place.
On your marks, get set, go!

It's the Pajama Jamma race!

And it was going quite well...
Until a shooting star hit me in the face.

The Pajama Jamma race led to outer space.

I touched the stars with my fingertips.

They felt like velvety potato chips.

Then I looked down
and realized I was standing
on a giraffe's head.
I slid down her neck
and landed on my bed...
only to be greeted by
Party Monsters...

Riding around

THERE'S A FEW THINGS ABOUT BEDTIME THAT NO ONE IN THE WORLD KNOWS.

I'M GOING TO TELL YOU THOSE SECRETS, SO LISTEN UP CLOSE.

The robot's favorite sport just happens to be golf.

Bedbugs

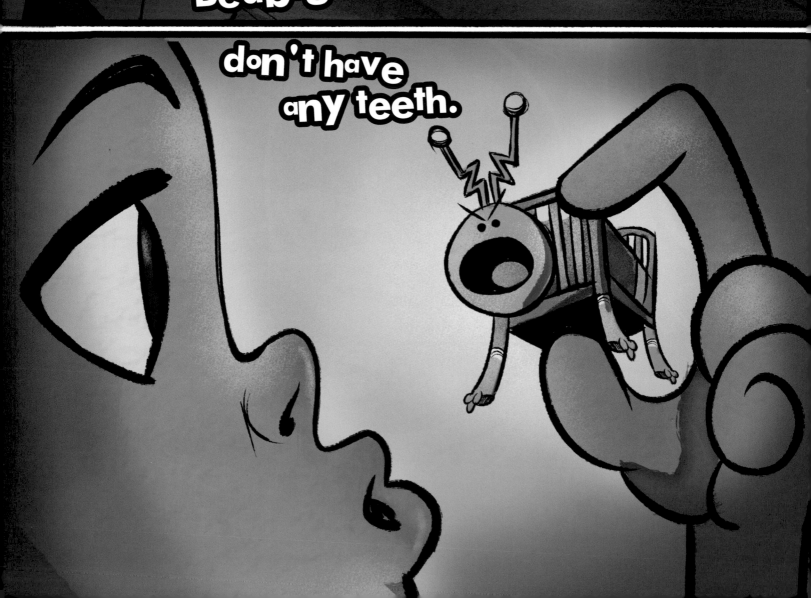

don't have any teeth.

And sometimes, just sometimes, magic happens while you sleep.

So I did the thing
that most parents dislike

And screamed with all my might,
in the middle of the night...

"THERE'S A PARTY IN MY ROOM, AND NO ONE WANTS TO LEAVE! IT'S TOTALLY OUT OF CONTROL. THESE MERMAIDS SPEAK PORTUGUESE. I DON'T UNDERSTAND ANYTHING THAT THEY'RE SAYING. I JUST WANT TO SLEEP. PLEASE! PLEASE. DADDDDYYY!!!"

But nothing seemed to have life when he turned on the lights.

ESpecially on nights when you really need rest.

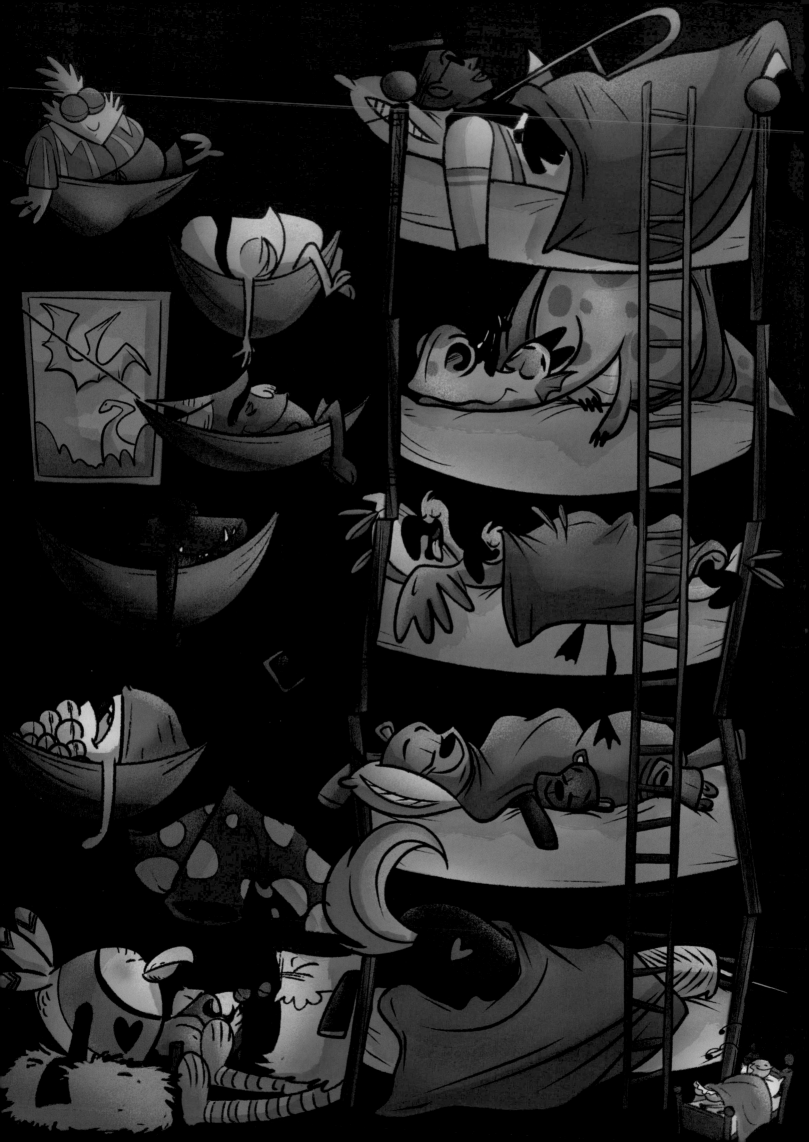

GOODNIGHT

The party's not over yet!
Join the after party by downloading A.J.'s brand new fun-tastic 'Hey A.J. It's Bedtime' app.

Party activities include:

- Collect A.J's Party Badges
- Pillow Fights
- Pizza Eating Dinosaurs
- Dancing Zombies
- Making S'mores
- Monster Smashing
- Story Time with Marty & Friends
- And Surprise Musical Gues[ts]

To discover A.J.'s amazing new app, search 'Hey AJ' in the app store.

www.theimaginationagency.com - www.heyaj.com
First published in USA by THE IMAGINATION AGENCY in 2017
ISBN: 978-0-9969820-2-3

Text copyright © Martellus Bennett 2017 - Illustrations copyright © Balloon Dog, LLC 2017
The author and illustrator assert the moral right to be identified as the author and illustrator of the work.

Book design Digital Leaf - Printed in China

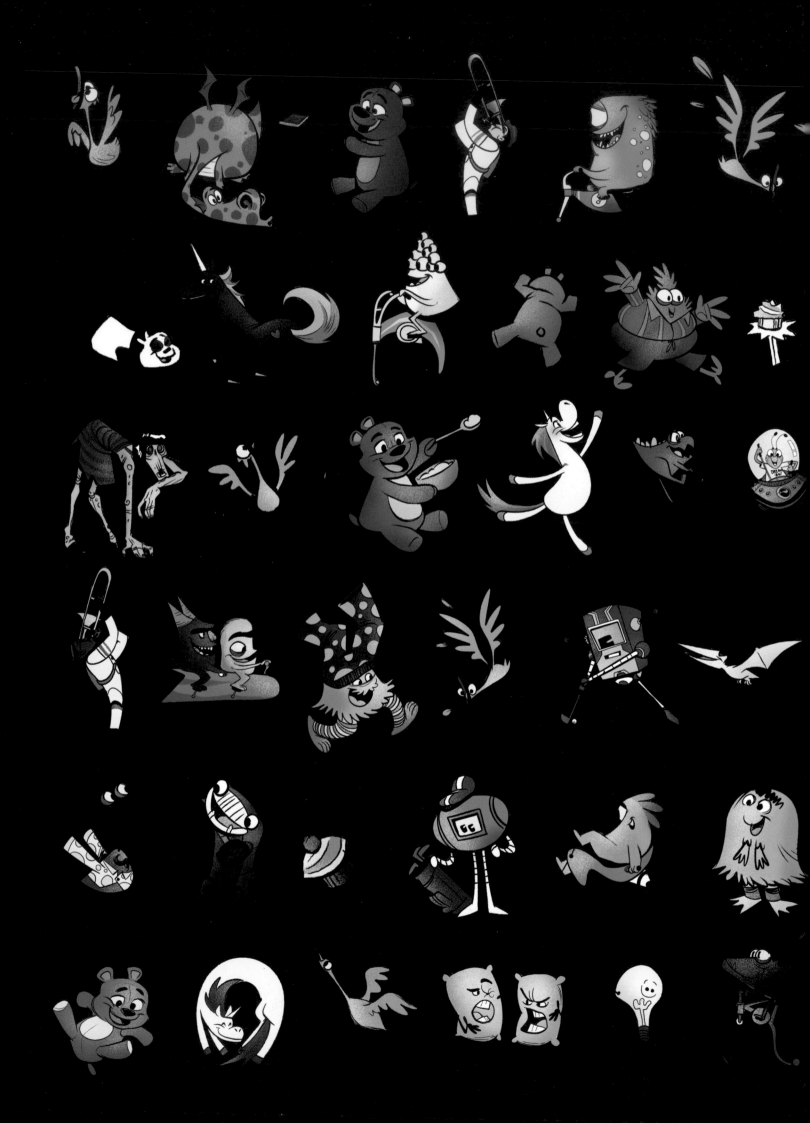